Mary Moon
Is
MISSING

The Adventures of Minnie and Max

Also in this series:

Minnie and Max

Mary Moon Is MISSING

Patricia Reilly Giff

illustrated by
Lynne Cravath

VIKING

Love and welcome to
Patricia Johanna O'Meara
March 25, 1998

Thank you to Diane Batemarco
for her research into the world of pigeons

Thank you to Alice Giff O'Meara
who makes fingerprint cookies every Christmas

VIKING
Published by the Penguin Group
Penguin Putnam Books for Young Readers, 345 Hudson Street, New York,
New York 10014, U.S.A.
Penguin Books Ltd, 27 Wrights Lane, London W8 5TZ, England
Penguin Books Australia Ltd, Ringwood, Victoria, Australia
Penguin Books Canada Ltd, 10 Alcorn Avenue, Toronto, Ontario, Canada M4V 3B2
Penguin Books (N.Z.) Ltd, 182-190 Wairau Road, Auckland 10, New Zealand

Penguin Books Ltd, Registered Offices: Harmondsworth, Middlesex, England

First published in 1998 by Viking, a member of Penguin Putnam Books for Young Readers.

1   3   5   7   9   10   8   6   4   2

Text copyright © Patricia Reilly Giff, 1998
Illustrations copyright © Lynne Cravath, 1998
All rights reserved

LIBRARY OF CONGRESS CATALOGING-IN-PUBLICATION DATA
Giff, Patricia Reilly.
Mary Moon is missing / Patricia Reilly Giff ; illustrated by Lynne Cravath.
p. cm.—(The adventures of Minnie and Max ; #2)
Summary : Assisted by her cat Max and her friend Cash, Minnie tries to find Mary Moon,
a valuable racing pigeon that has disappeared just before a big race.
ISBN 0-670-88182-1
[1. Racing pigeons—Fiction. 2. Pigeons—Fiction. 3. Cats—Fiction. 4. Mystery and
detective stories.] I. Cravath, Lynne Woodcock, ill. II. Title. III. Series: Giff, Patricia Reilly.
Adventures of Minnie and Max ; #2.
PZ7.G3626Mar 1998 [Fic]—dc21   98-15554   CIP   AC

Printed in U.S.A.   Set in Sabon

CONTENTS

MYSTERY

It was hot, it was steamy, it was summer. My cat Max and I were mushing along Emmons Avenue, on our way to Minnow Beach.

"This is it, Minnie," Captain Ted shouted over from Pier Three.

"What's it?" I was almost too hot to ask; too hot to think. The sun was beating down on my straw hat, through my bangs, boring a hole into my brain.

"The Pigeon Prize Race on Saturday," said old Ted, sloshing a pail of water across the filthy deck of his boat.

I used one of my last drops of energy to nod. To tell the truth, I wasn't into pigeons. I was into mysteries.

I did know that someone in a boat would take the racing pigeons to Weed Island in airy little boxes, and let them go. I knew the pigeons would zoom home to their nests, their mates, their children . . . and that the fastest zoomer would win five hundred bucks for his owner.

You'd have to be a stick of wood not to know. Flags

were flying everywhere, ribbons fluttering, people talking pigeons, practicing pigeons, praying for a win.

I used up another drop of energy to wave at the captain, and then Max and I turned onto the bridge. I made believe I was in a desert. "Water," I moaned.

Max padded along in back of me. He wasn't worried about water. He could always find a puddle.

Right now, we were looking for a mystery. Actually, we had been looking for a week. Max and I were in the business. The detective business. *You Lose, I Find*. Great name, right? We had just about given up on a new case when we decided to see how Casmir was doing. He was smart, he was my friend, and he was in the business, too.

"Listen, Max," I said. "We won't tell Cash we're ready to horn in on one of his mysteries. We'll play it cool, you know? Sound bored."

Max wasn't paying attention. He was working on a lump of lemon swirl ice cream someone had dropped on the bridge.

Just then I heard the sound of wheels galumphing across the bridge: patrol car wheels from the Sixty-first Precinct. Yes. I recognized the dent in the front fender. It was the Klutz, Officer Kitty Kirov. Off duty, she was my brother Orlando's girlfriend and part-time cook at the Catfish Cafe. No wonder. She was gorgeous, with dark curly hair, tight to her head, and sky blue eyes. Not only that, she was a great cop.

Right now her arm was out the window; she was tapping her red-striped nails on the car roof, humming along with a song in her head, probably "Pet-toon-ya You're My Piddgg-yonn." She'd been singing that all week.

She waved when she saw us. "The best news, Minnie," she told me.

I fanned my face with my hand. "A mystery?"

She shook her head. "Better."

"Hmmm," I said, losing interest fast.

"You'll see, it's good," she told me. "I'm coming over to the restaurant as soon as I'm off duty. Tell you then."

"No fair," I said.

"That's life." She grinned.

And that was the beginning of a mystery, a great mystery, even though Max and I didn't know it then: Kitty's news; an hour later, Mary Moon; and the strange things that would happen in the next few days. They'd all work into a puzzle, a puzzle we'd have to solve.

But for the moment, I was waiting for Max to finish his lemon ice cream. Then we headed for the sand and the water, feeling hot, feeling sticky.

If only we had known.

2

MINNOW BEACH

I thought about the ocean's icy coldness; I thought I'd swim around for an hour before I looked for my friend Cash.

And that's what I did. I took a flying leap into the Atlantic and came up sputtering. I tried to ignore Max, who was darting back and forth at the water's edge.

Max was frantic. Max hated the ocean. Worse, he hated it when I was bobbing around in it. I guess he felt guilty because he wasn't trying to save my life. After all, Max and I were a team, dawn to dusk, night to morning.

Anyway, I floated just under the surface, coming up once in a while to wave, then I took pity on him and dragged myself out of the surf to search for Cash. It wasn't hard. Cash had stretched his skinny self out on a blanket at the edge of the surf. Both his feet were in the water, and his mouth was filled with Oreo cookies.

Max and I tiptoed up until we were so close we could see the freckles on his nose. Then we pounced. We dived onto his wet, sandy blanket and grabbed for the cookies.

"Pathetic." Cash held his bag away from us. "I saw your shadows a mile away."

"What's up?" I asked, hardly missing a beat.

He pushed the bag over to me. "Nothing."

"Not that I care," For a moment, I glanced down at my shriveled fingers. Too bad. By the time I raised my head, I had only one quick look at the beige carrier pigeon. He was flying toward Sharkfin Bay, carrying a capsule in his harness. The harness must have been loose. Suddenly, the capsule dropped . . .

. . . into the foam and seaweed at the water's edge.

Max got to it first, patting it with one dainty paw. Cash grabbed it next, turning it over in his fingers.

Then it was my turn. I could see that the bullet-shaped container was actually two halves screwed together. I twisted it, the sandy edges grating before it opened. "Something's inside," I muttered.

"Money," said Cash. "We're rich."

"Don't be pathetic. It's paper." I dug at the tiny piece with wet fingers, pulling at it, smoothing it on my knee, and began to read:

HELP—DESPERATE
Mary Moon is missing
Prize pigeon

I never read the rest of it, because Max was on my knees, digging his sharp claws into my leg, sniffing at the paper. Cash was leaning over my shoulder . . .

. . . and the tide was rising. I could feel the spray from the water. I scrunched back as three kids came barreling across the sand. They were yelling at each other, laughing, so I didn't get to hear what Cash said next.

I saw, though. Cash scrambled up, staring up at the

wave that was coming in on us like a locomotive. I grabbed Max and the bag of cookies and slid backwards as fast as I could.

Not fast enough.

The wave wasn't a locomotive, it was a rocket, sweeping all of us into the ocean. Cat, cookies, Cash, me . . .

. . . and the carrier pigeon's message.

We all rode the next wave in. Then Cash and I took deep breaths. We floated face down, eyes open, searching. We dived. We swam along the bottom, our hands stretched out like starfish, while Max ran back and forth on the shore, meowing.

A half hour later, skin scraped raw from sand, shells, and a vicious little jellyfish, we had to give up.

The paper was gone, heading out to sea.

3

MUSIC

My brother Orlando was dashing around the kitchen of our restaurant, The Catfish Cafe. He stirred a pot of soup. He checked the mousse in the refrigerator. He popped a tiny potato ball into my mouth.

"Ooh-la-la," I said, after I swallowed.

"New recipe," Orlando said. I could tell he was pleased that I liked it.

Orlando was my whole family. We stuck together like glue. The only time it ever got a little sticky was when he bossed me around. He bossed because he was a worrier. I didn't boss. Orlando was too big for me to worry about. But the truth was I was crazy about him, and I knew he was crazy about me.

But enough of that. It was time for the salad. I reached for a head of lettuce and started to tear it into skinny little shreds. I took a breath. Somehow I had caught a cold. I tried not to sneeze.

One sneeze out of me and Orlando would be feeling my forehead for a fever, thinking about the flu or even the plague.

I finished up the salad. Then I pushed through the swinging door and went out to the front. The Catfish Cafe was open for dinner.

Against one wall was the most terrific player piano you've ever seen. Orlando and I had fished it out of the dump last week, borrowed Lumber Jack's truck, and lugged it home.

Orlando was great at fiddling with wires. He'd fiddled us into having the best player piano in Sharkfin Bay. He just hadn't figured out how to make it play without banging into it.

I punched A-2, shoved my hip into the side to start the action, and watched as the keys began to move by themselves. Presto. "Pet-toon-ya You're My Piddgg-yon."

I went back into the kitchen, wondering about Kitty's news, but I didn't find out until much later. From seven o'clock on, the restaurant was jumping. Max watched the customers from his perch on the cash register, while I ran around like a madwoman with the silverware.

Kitty the Klutz was dropping, spilling, clanking silver, but managing to cook the best Russian chicken anyone had ever tasted. And Orlando was trying to serve twenty customers at once.

Over in a corner, I spotted Tough Teresa. She was scarfing up a pile of chicken legs. Three things about Teresa. She was seventeen, she had a loft full of racing pigeons, and she deserved her own prize for disgusting table manners. Oh, and one more thing, Teresa hated cats. Not so surprising, I guess. Cats and pigeons were a bad mix.

Tough Teresa. I blinked. Teresa might know something about our pigeon mystery.

But I didn't have time for a mystery. I was scurrying in back of Orlando with ice water and spoons. Never mind the spoons, I told myself, edging over to Teresa's table.

"So how's it going, Teresa?" I set the pitcher down with a clunk and slid into the empty seat opposite her.

Orlando caught sight of me and almost had a fit. It was easy to tell. Orlando's mustache was twitching to beat the band. When he was calm, it lay there like a fat brush, moving gently as he chewed on the edge of it.

I pretended it was a fat brush and turned my back. "The word is there's a missing pigeon," I told Teresa.

Teresa looked at me quickly, a chicken leg dangling from her mouth. "Wrong word." She dumped the bare little bone on top of a pile, acting as if chicken was the only thing on her mind. But I had seen her jump.

"A prize pigeon," I said, stopping for a quick sneeze. "She's probably going to win the race on Saturday."

"Billy the Kid is going to win the Pigeon Prize Race," Teresa said in a voice loud enough for the whole restaurant

to hear. "*My* pigeon." She pointed to her chest with a gravy-stained finger. "Fastest bird on the bay."

I stared at her. Teresa was lying about something. I was getting good at telling things like that. Kitty had taught me. Body language, she called it. When a person wiggled around when he talked, when he didn't look you straight in the eye: *bam, wrong-o, caught.*

"The pigeon's name is Mary Moon," I said.

Now Teresa really jumped. But this time she grabbed my wrist hard. I tried to pull away, but she was leaning forward, glaring. "Keep out of this pigeon business," she said. "I'm warning you. You might end up getting killed . . . or worse."

I couldn't think of anything worse. I swallowed while Teresa scooped up a leg with each hand. Then Orlando was back, his mustache twitching. "The piano stopped ten minutes ago," he said.

I skittered out of the chair as fast as I could. My wrist was red, my heart was racing. I went over to the piano and began to look for another song, trying to calm myself. We'd had enough "Pet-toon-ya You're My Piddgg-yon" for one night.

At that moment, Kitty came out of the kitchen wearing her tall white chef's hat. She leaned over my shoulder, pressed O-5, punched the top of the piano, and gave me a bear hug.

Orlando came over. He put one arm around Kitty and one arm around me. He was smiling. And when Orlando smiled, he was a knockout.

Then the music blared out; Kitty sang along: *"We're going to get ma-aaaa-ried."*

And that's how I learned about Kitty's news. Kitty and Orlando's news, I should say.

We were going to have an engagement party at the Catfish Cafe, on the day of the Pigeon Prize Race.

4

MESSAGE

I tossed and turned all night. I woke up to sneeze. I woke up to blow my nose. I woke up to think about something Kitty had told me. Take anything you know about a case, find out about it, and sooner or later, presto!

What did I know? One, Mary Moon was missing.

Find out more about pigeons, I told myself. I could ask Ryan Biale, a guy with a pile of pigeons in his coop.

Two, that brat, Tough Teresa, had warned me to forget about Mary Moon. I rubbed my wrist.

Find out more about that brat, Tough Teresa, I told myself next. I'd think of how later.

I sat up and stretched. It was time to get up anyway. And then I thought of something. I had only four bucks for an engagement present. Good grief. I threw myself against my pillow and landed on Max's tail. "Sorry," I said, still trying to think. Pigeon, Teresa, present. I began again. Pigeon . . . Yes. Bird Berry.

"Bird Berry," I said aloud. "The pigeon lady." I closed my eyes thinking about her. If you stood on the Minnow Beach Bridge and looked out at Muck Island, you'd see a patch of green, a patch of tan, and a bit of the patched-up cabin that belonged to Bird and her pigeons.

Orlando loved Bird. She had taken care of us for awhile until Orlando had grown up.

Orlando would never think of Bird's coming all the way from Muck Island.

If I could sneak her into the engagement party . . .

"What a present," I told Max as I climbed out of bed and threw on my clothes. "I'm a genius."

I stopped for a quick breakfast of cold potato balls and juice. Good thing Orlando was out on the piers buying fish for tonight's dinner. Orlando was into breakfast food and vitamins for me.

From the window I could see the piers. Sonny Breitenback, a teenager from down near Pier Three, had opened his pigeon loft. Sonny was into tumblers. A bunch flew out and up over Sharkfin Bay.

I waited, munching on a potato ball. Sonny was waiting, too, his hands in his pockets, probably with a clove of garlic his grandmother made him carry to ward off colds. I'd rather have the cold, I thought.

Suddenly, one of Sonny's black-and-white pigeons began to roll, trying to touch its tail with the back of its head.

A second started. Then they were all tumbling in the sky as they gained height. Sonny's pigeons were high fliers, not racers. A moment later, they were just specks beneath the clouds.

I shook my head. I was wasting time. I had to meet the ferry. I slid into my sneakers and burst out of the Catfish Cafe, with Max coming after me.

Cash met us at the corner, looking as if he'd melt in the sun. "What's up?"

"The best engagement present in the world for Orlando and Kitty."

"Money," he said. "You're going to win the Pigeon Prize Race and give it to them."

"Pathetic," I said, out of breath. "I don't even have a pigeon."

We skittered onto the pier. A hot wind was blowing the pigeon flags and ribbons around, and the line of wash strung out on the deck of the *Michael T. Moriarty*. Captain Ted called it a ferry; everyone else called it a mess. Someday that boat would settle down in the water and not stop settling until it sank to the bottom. But it was the only thing afloat that puttered its way over to Muck Island and Bird Berry.

It set out every Monday, stopping at one island after another, then looped its way back on Friday.

We made it just in time. Captain Ted was untying the ropes that held the *Michael T. Moriarty* to the pier. He peered over his half-glasses, his watch cap down over his eyebrows.

I waved my letter to Bird at him. "Will you take this to Bird?" I asked. "Bring her back on Friday with you?"

He shoved his glasses up. "Sure."

I stood there as he hopped onto the boat with the letter in his hand. I hoped this wasn't the week the *Moriarty* would fall apart.

I yanked on Cash's shoulder. "We have a mystery to solve," I said, "and a date with Ryan Biale." I couldn't help grinning. I sounded like a real detective.

We stopped at Food Fair first. Everyone knew Ryan loved candy, a Hershey's bar, a handful of jelly beans. Then we had a long climb, up the street, up the ladder on the side of his garage, onto the roof, and there he was. A pale gray pigeon was perched on one shoulder, pecking at his earlobe. About twenty others lined the top of the coop, preening their feathers.

"Mary Moon . . ." I began. My voice didn't even sound like mine. I must be losing my voice, I thought. I handed him a chocolate bar.

Ryan peeled back the candy wrapper, and shoved half the bar into his mouth.

"She's a prize pigeon," I said, coughing.

He shook his head, thinking. "Never heard of her. Going to put her in the big race on Saturday?

"Not our pigeon," I said.

Down below, locked out of the loft, Max was crying.

Ryan pointed to one of the pigeons. "I'm going to race that one. Sweet Patootie."

I looked up. There were so many pigeons—beige ones, and gray ones, even one that looked yellow.

He took another bite of candy and smiled. "I never won a race before. But this time I know I'm going to win." He held out what was left of the candy. Almost nothing. "Want a bite?" he asked.

I shook my head.

Ryan looked up at the pigeons. "It's going to be great to be a winner. The greatest."

Then Cash and I listened as he told us about homing pigeons. "Not your ordinary pigeon," he said. "Homers are smart. They race to get home, and they race fast. The best ones can do five hundred miles in a day."

"But why would one be missing?" I asked.

Ryan swallowed the last bite. He looked sad. "A hawk might have grabbed her," he said. "Or maybe she flew into a wire."

Cash and I looked at each other. "Horrible," I said.

"Sometimes they're so exhausted, they'll stop to rest somewhere." He raised one shoulder. "For days."

I heard a whirring of wings as a pigeon flew up and settled back on the roof. I looked back. Inside the coop, I could see two or three birds still in cages.

"Why . . ." I began, pointing.

Ryan reached behind me and closed the door. "Off their feed," he said. "They need a day or two of quiet."

"Suppose someone kidnapped a pigeon, kidnapped Mary Moon, maybe?" I said slowly. "Suppose he held onto her until after the race?"

Ryan was still chewing, but Cash was right with me. "Then another pigeon would win," Cash said. "Maybe a pigeon who wasn't so fast."

"I guess so. Sure. That could happen." Ryan checked out the empty wrapper for bits of chocolate. He patted up a few crumbs with one damp finger. "Mary Moon," he said, shaking his head. "If she was that good, that fast, I think I would have heard about her."

Cash took two steps to the coop. "Mind if I see them?"

Ryan was sucking on the edge of the wrapper now. He jerked his head a little toward me. "I'm really sorry, but Minnie has a cold, and . . ."

I nodded, but I was thinking of something else. If Mary Moon had been kidnapped, we had to find her right away. Suppose Ryan was wrong? Suppose she was fast enough to win the race.

I thought about Tough Teresa saying I could be killed— or worse. Then I shook my head. Never mind Teresa. Looking for Mary Moon was the right thing to do.

5

MIDNIGHT

I loved Sharkfin Bay. I loved the water and the boats. I could dive down deep where it was dark, and cold, and not be one bit afraid. But sneaking around at night was another thing. And sneaking around while I had the world's worst cold was still another.

It had to be done, though. Tough Teresa's coop was the only clue we had.

I waited around in my room while Orlando took forever to get himself to bed. He must have spent an hour brushing his teeth, trimming his mustache, singing, *"We're going to get ma-aaaa-ried"* in his deep voice. *"Minnie's going to be the maid of honor and the best maaaaan."*

I was waiting for Max to get to sleep, too. This was no case for Max. I shuddered to think of Max padding around in a pigeon coop.

At last, Orlando stopped singing and Max stopped purring. Everyone was asleep. I pushed up the screen an inch at a time and peered out. Cash was slinking around at

20

the end of the alley, blinking a flashlight to signal me.

I clambered up and over the sill, suddenly feeling Max's sharp little claws on my shoulder. Before I could grab him, he was down the alley ahead of us. He stopped to scarf up a dead killie, then skipped along checking over his shoulder to be sure we were going his way. And we were. Max knew exactly where we were going.

It took us five minutes. There was no moon, exactly as it said in mystery books, so that was our first piece of luck. The second piece of luck was that Teresa hadn't bothered to lock the back window of her garage. Not surprising. No one in his right mind would sneak around in a yard full of poison ivy, poison oak, and sumac.

No one but Cash and Max and me.

Max sat waiting on Teresa's window looking like the cat who had swallowed the canary, or in this case, the cat who had eaten the killie. "Wait right here," I told him.

He glared at us with lollipop yellow eyes, but stayed on the sill as we climbed over him and into the garage. In the darkness, the circular staircase to the roof was a bulky shape in the corner, a giant, bending and twisting. I could feel my heart begin to pound. Why was I doing something like this? I wondered. I walked across the room, careful not to bump into anything or stumble over the boxes of pigeon food that were lying around.

In back of Cash, I grabbed the railing and climbed, hearing the muffled hum of a motorboat on the bay. I could see

21

lights from the window. I leaned over, staring out. It was a patrol car from the Sixty-first Precinct. I didn't know whether to be scared or glad.

And then we were at the top. We pushed back the trapdoor that led to the roof, and pulled ourselves out. The moon was coming up over the bay now. I could see the Big Dipper. I could see the pigeon coop.

Cash pulled out his flashlight and snapped it on. Then we opened the door to the coop quietly, listening to the small rustle of feathers. Sleepy pigeons nested in boxes that lined the walls. The boxes were immaculate, and so was the floor.

Cash was whispering. "You see the bands on their legs? When the pigeons are born, their back claws fold easily. The owner can slide the band up over one of their legs. Later, the claw won't bend, so the band will never come off. Each bird has his own number."

I nodded. We were walking from one box to another. There were labels on some: ANNIE OAKLEY, JESSIE JAMES, and ASTEROID. Next came BILLY THE KID. I stopped to stare. That was the pigeon Teresa had said would win Saturday's race. The pigeon stared back at me with glassy red eyes, every feather in place.

"Look," I said to Cash.

Cash leaned over my shoulder.

Billy was quiet, still. It didn't seem to bother him that we were there. A champion, I thought. The other pigeons were awake now, disturbed, cooing and clucking and flapping

their wings. "Maybe we should go," I said uneasily.

Downstairs I heard a door slam. We looked at each other. "We'll go over the next roof," Cash said.

I took a breath, ready to run. But then we saw it, both of us at the same time. "The pigeon isn't moving at all." I poked my finger gently through the wire.

Next to me, Cash's eyes were huge. "It's not alive."

"It's stuffed," I said. "Just an old stuffed pigeon."

"But why?" we both said at once.

We could hear footsteps now. We raced along the row of cages, going toward the back of the roof as lights came on, huge lights that lit up the roofs like the Fourth of July on Coney Island.

I ducked down, scampering across the gluey surface of tar ahead of Cash. I barreled along full speed . . .

. . . and tripped on my sneaker laces. I landed on knees, elbows, and chin. My teeth snapped together so hard I could feel the top one chip a little. I had a quick flash of myself at the engagement party: toothless. And then I felt a small round disc under my hand. A dime? I shoved it into my pocket, feeling I had to sneeze. Don't sneeze, I told myself, trying to hear what was happening below.

We could hear a voice now, Teresa's. Cash helped me scramble to my feet. We took off, hopping across to the next garage and down the outside steps of the next building. Then I heard something else. It was the yowl of a cat. My cat, Max.

6

MAX

We went back, of course. I couldn't leave Max to be thrown into the bay or into a pot of Teresa's pigeon-feed stew. But the lights were out; everything was still.

I called softly, "Max?" And called again. Cash and I kept calling for twenty minutes. Then, with a heavy feeling in my chest, I headed for home. Cash kept looking at me. I knew he was trying to think of something to say. He knew how terrible I felt. I left him at Emmons Avenue, telling myself Max would have beaten me home, telling myself he was curled up in the huge blue mixing bowl in the kitchen, or on the pillow in my bed.

I tiptoed through the kitchen, sweeping my hand around the bowl, and then went into my bedroom. It was a good thing I knew where everything was. I couldn't see a thing through my tears.

I sat on the edge of the bed. Should I go back again? But if Max were a prisoner, I'd never be able to find him tonight. If he had escaped he'd be home in a flash. I opened the screen wide enough for him to come through. I kept thinking about that stuffed bird. Why would Teresa have put him in a cage? Why would she have said he'd win the race?

I peeled off my shorts and shirt and tossed them on the chair. Something rolled across the floor, probably the dime from Teresa's roof.

I pulled on my pajamas and climbed into bed, feeling miserable. I hoped Max was alive. I hoped I'd wake in the morning fighting for the pillow. I hoped . . .

The next thing I knew it was light. Across the way, fishing boats were gearing up, ready to head for open water. And in my bedroom, I was alone. Max hadn't come home.

I reached for my clothes. And then I saw the dime on the floor, except that it wasn't a dime at all. I bent down to pick it up. It was a button: thin, silvery, and looking familiar. I went over to my dresser. There was a picture Bird had sent us last summer. She was wearing a summer dress, mint green with silver buttons. Yes, the button matched.

I sat there turning it over in my hand, feeling its smoothness. It was almost like touching Bird's cheek.

I closed my eyes. I pictured the *Michael T. Moriarty* chugging up to Bird's dock. I pictured her running around giving her pigeons piles of food, then pulling out her dress for the party.

I opened my eyes. I was supposed to go shopping for a dress for the engagement party. After all I was going to be the maid of honor, *and* best man at the wedding. I was planning on a purple deluxe outfit.

I swallowed. How could I do that? I had to find Max. And thought again. How could I tell Kitty and Orlando that Max was missing? How could I say we'd been skulking around in the middle of the night, raiding Tough Teresa's pigeon coop?

I finished dressing, thinking about it. I wouldn't say a word about Max. I knew Cash would keep looking. I'd go with Kitty, grab the first decent dress I spotted, and be back to search in an hour.

And that's what I did. I mean, that's what I almost did. Orlando had cooked up a special breakfast, blueberry pancakes, in honor of the shopping day, and tons of fresh orange juice for my cold. And then I started for the Sixty-first Precinct. Kitty would be off duty any minute and we'd hop in her jeep and head for GRAND STREET—GRAND GOWNS.

On the way, I saw Sonny Breitenback leaning against the Pier Twelve railing. "Seen a cat?" I asked.

He shook his head, smelling of garlic.

"Seen a pigeon?"

"Tons of them." He grinned.

"Mary Moon?" I said.

"What's this, twenty questions?" He scrunched up his nose. "Heard of her, haven't seen her."

I kept going, but I didn't even get to the corner. Kitty was barreling along in her jeep, waving out the window. I slid inside, sniffling, and tried to sing along with her, even though I couldn't stop thinking of Max. *"We're going to get maaaa-rrriiieeed . . ."*

After a minute, she stopped. "The dessert for the engagement party," she said. "It has to be different. It has to be . . ."

"Delicious," I said.

"Something to do with . . ."

I tried to think. "Pigeons?"

She shook her head. "Hmmm. No."

We started across Minnow Beach Bridge. Red and blue ribbons were fluttering from the crossbars. And then I felt my heart lurch. "Stop," I yelled.

Kitty slammed on the brakes and I was out of my seat belt, out of the car, because Max was there, right there on the bridge railing, smiling at me.

Really.

He flicked his tail once and kept looking at a pigeon who was perched on the very top crossbar.

I grabbed Max, hugged him, and slid back into the car. We were off to buy a marvelous purple dress and a matching collar for Max.

I never did think about the pigeon again until after lunch.

7

MISSTEP

Cash was hanging out on the pier waiting while I hung my gorgeous purple dress in the closet.

"It's probably an old Sharkfin Bay type of pigeon taking a rest," I said when I caught up with him. "But suppose . . ."

"Did it have a band on its leg?" he asked. "A detective would have noticed."

"Do you think I have X-ray eyes?" I glared at him, thinking he was right.

Max was dancing around between us, begging to be noticed.

I glanced down at him. "Why was Max looking at that pigeon?" I asked slowly. "Staring at it?"

"Pigeon pie," said Cash.

I shook my head. "Forty million pigeons hang around, dropping seeds and feathers and you-know-what. He never even pays attention to them."

Max was marching back and forth, eyes alert, tail up.

"We have to take ourselves over to the bridge," I said.

"Now." I sped through the kitchen gathering up a bagful of bagel chips. Orlando wouldn't mind. Orlando wouldn't know. He was at the library reading about Russian wedding desserts.

By the time we could see the bridge, we were hot and sticky. Max jumped up on the railing first, and we were right after him, looking up, our fingers crossed. And high overhead was the pigeon, staring down at us. She had a silvery band around one leg.

"She's tired," Cash and I said at the same time. We were thinking about what Ryan had told us about homing pigeons. *Sometimes they're so exhausted, they'll stop to rest somewhere. For days.*

Max went up first, hopping daintily to the next crossbar.

"Listen, Max," I said, reaching for him. "Why don't you go home? Orlando will be sautéing scallops for dinner any minute." True. "You can nab a couple for a treat." Probably not true, but I was desperate.

Max wasn't having any of it. He was looking up at the pigeon, and maybe it was Mary Moon. Good grief. Maybe he'd nab Mary for a treat if I didn't do something fast.

I grabbed him and held him tight as we waited for a truck to galumph by, then I scattered the chips around. "Here, Mary," I cooed.

I couldn't tell if she saw the chips or heard me call. Her eyes were half closed. She'd never come down to the floor of the bridge anyway, not with Max waiting to pounce.

"This isn't going to work," I said.

Cash looked at Max. "Vamoose. Scat," he said. "Hide."

Max staring at us with his yellow eyes. He knew what we were talking about; he always knew. He pretended his feelings were hurt, and stalked away toward the rocks below the bridge.

"Coo, coo," I called, but the pigeon didn't move. Maybe she couldn't move. Maybe she was stuck up there.

Just then a car went by and flattened the chips. The bird moved. She flew off the bridge like a rocket. She was so fast she was almost a blur. And then she swooped back and landed, almost in the same spot.

I looked up at her. We had no bait now, so I'd have to climb. My hands felt wet thinking about how high that was. Just suppose I reached the top and fell? Suppose I reached the top and the pigeon flew?

I had a quick picture of Bird Berry in my mind. Bird, who loved pigeons. "Cover their eyes and they won't move," she had told me once.

I needed a bit of cloth, a piece of towel. How about my T-shirt: MINNIE'S DETECTIVE AGENCY. YOU LOSE. I FIND. Good thing I had my bathing suit on underneath. I peeled off the shirt and began to climb.

Well, not exactly. I looked up first to see the best way of becoming a sky diver. I'd have to go from crossbar to crossbar, and if I missed, I'd go straight into the bay. I boosted myself up about an inch, trying to find room for my feet.

High above, the pigeon was watching me, and just under-neath me, Cash was biting his fingernails.

On the rocks, Max was keeping one eye on me, the other on a pile of mussels. Max wouldn't be worried. His idea of a perfect afternoon was a perch in the swaying chandelier of the Catfish Cafe.

I took a breath, thinking about taking the next step. I counted—there were ten crossbars. Ribbons hanging from the bars kept getting in my eyes, tickling my nose. I could see the water below, blue and sparkling, and the turtle shape of Muck Island in the distance with its sandy beach and green scrub trees. I stared at a piece of Bird's cabin. I wondered what she'd think if she knew I was thinking about climbing to the nearest cloud. "Go for it," she'd say. Bird was into trying things.

It took me twenty minutes to think about climbing the first crossbar. That wasn't counting a stop to sneeze. It wasn't counting the little screaming argument I had with a motorist who yelled out his window that I was a menace trying to kill myself and good luck to the pedestrians.

And by this time, there were plenty of pedestrians waiting to see if I'd climb. "This is pathetic," Cash whispered, a foot below me. "Are you going to do it or not?"

"She thinks she's in the circus," a woman with a know-it-all face said.

"Call the police," some busybody joined in. "Nine-one-one."

Good grief. That's all I needed. "Don't worry," I said. "My almost sister-in-law is a cop. Besides, I haven't gone anywhere yet."

That didn't stop them. They were fuming, and fussing, trying to think of what to do about me.

I squinted up in the sunlight. I could see the pigeon's feathers, soft with dark arrows on the edges, and her bright orange eyes. I reached for the next crossbar, and . . .

Missed. I could feel myself sliding and tried to grab it, but the bars seemed slippery now, and so were my hands.

"There she goes, into the water," screamed Busybody. "I knew it." She was wrong. I grabbed the steel girder and hung on as if my life depended on it. It was a little ridiculous, I thought. I could have jumped to the bridge floor without a problem. Going higher was the problem.

I took four deep breaths. I could see Tough Teresa, her mouth wrapped around a hamburger the size of a soccer ball, and then I saw Sonny Breitenback coming along. I closed my eyes, hugging the girder, leaning into it.

"What's that idiot trying to do?" Tough Teresa said.

I opened my eyes. In one move, Teresa had scaled the railing. I saw what she was going to do. She was going to climb and grab the pigeon for herself. She had to show she was tougher than I was.

She *was* tougher than I was.

I hoisted myself up another inch. I made cooing sounds. "Here pidgie, pidgie," I said.

"Pathetic," Cash said again.

The pigeon looked at me. She looked at Teresa. And then by some wonderful piece of luck, she swooped down, past Teresa's outstretched arms, and landed on my head.

I reached up with one hand, slowly, carefully, and guided her down, cuddling her against my chest.

Everyone was cheering now, even Know-It-All and Busybody.

Everyone but Orlando, who was racing along Emmons Avenue, heading for the bridge, heading for me.

I tried a quick bow from the lowest crossbar, then I leaned over as far as I could to hand the bird to Cash. I took a breath, and dropped into the bay below, holding my T-shirt over my head like a flag.

8

MISTAKE

Jumping into the bay didn't do one bit of good. Orlando was standing at the edge, jeans and sneakers soaked. He looked as if his mustache would fly off his lip. He looked as if he was about to burst into tears.

He marched me straight back to the restaurant, with Cash following, but not too close. No one wanted to get near Orlando when he was having hysterics.

"With a cold like that—" Orlando began, as if that had to do with anything.

"I just wanted to capture—" I began, reaching back to take the pigeon from Cash.

"Don't think you're bringing that bird in my restaurant."

"*Our* restaurant." I swept in ahead of him, "I'll be right out," I told Cash. I pressed L-3, and slapped the piano. "And I'm bringing Mary Moon into *my* room," I told Orlando over the music of "You're a Grand Old Flag."

"Mary Moon," Orlando said. "I can't stand it." He

35

went into the kitchen to bang pots and pans around. "Scallops burnt to a cinder," he muttered. "Who knows what tonight's special will be? And don't ever go up on that bridge again, Minnie."

I didn't answer, but Orlando was right. I didn't even want to think about that climb. And now that Mary was cooing gently in my arms. I didn't have to.

I could still hear Orlando talking to himself, saying he'd never forgive himself if I had ended up floating in the bay. I grinned. Orlando was a nervous wreck.

I set Mary down in the middle of the bed. A little hot, but it was nice and fluffy, with the quilt and sheet lumped up in a ball. She'd be fine right there until I got back. I climbed out the window and headed down the alley.

We had to find out what to feed a pigeon. We had to find out where she belonged. We had to get her ready for the race on Saturday.

And Ryan Biale was the guy to tell us how.

We scurried over to his pigeon coop, telling each other what nerve Tough Teresa had.

"She can't stand to see anyone else doing something cool like climbing a bridge," Cash said.

"Right," I said. "She has to be on top of the heap."

Cash grinned. "Top of the bridge."

We knocked on the door of the coop, a pile of chocolate bars in our hands. Ryan was there, a pigeon on his shoulder, and about ten more circling his head.

We told him about the bridge, and the message, we told him about Mary Moon. And in another ten minutes we were pigeon experts. At least, we knew she needed vitamins and fresh water, and Ryan had given us a bag of pigeon feed for her.

"What's her band number?" he asked.

I slapped my head. If I'd had a mustache, it would have vibrated. "I forgot to look," I said.

He nodded, his mouth filled with the chocolate bar we had brought him. "Tell me about her," he said.

I sneezed once, then I closed my eyes. I tried to remember every detail: her feathers, her cool little claws, her bright orange eyes. "She's fast," I said. "For a moment I saw her speed off the bridge."

"Hummm," he mumbled once, and "mmmm," after that. "But only for a moment?" he said.

I nodded and tried to think of something else. "Actually she looks regular," I said.

He shook his head at us. "That's what it sounds like . . . just a pigeon," he said, almost sadly. "Certainly not a prize pigeon."

"Not Mary Moon. A mistake." I could have cried, I was so disappointed. I thought back to climbing the bridge; I thought of the mess she was probably making of my sheets and quilt; I thought of the race money I was ready to share with the owner for finding her. Pathetic.

Ryan must have seen the look on my face. And Cash

looked just as sad. "Do you want me to take the pigeon?" Ryan asked. "I'll give it a good home."

But the pigeon seemed to fit with Max and me. Then I thought of something else, and my heart nearly stopped. I had forgotten about Max. He was probably up on my bed having a pigeon snack for himself.

I certainly couldn't tell that to Ryan. I ducked my head. "I think I'll hang onto the pigeon for a while."

I pinched Cash's arm to get him out of there fast, then we raced for my bedroom. I hoped we wouldn't have to set up a pigeon funeral for that afternoon.

9

MISCHIEF

A surprise was waiting for us. Two surprises, actually. Max and the pigeon were swinging from the chandelier in the restaurant.

It took us only a second to realize they were friends. How? Who knows? But there they were, Max and his meal, cooing, purring, snoozing, and there was nothing I could do to get them down.

I didn't even try. Cash left, customers came, Orlando cooked, Kitty served, and overhead, the chandelier swayed. No one even noticed. But I did, of course. The pigeon was building a nest out of my sun hat, and once in a while a bit of straw would float down onto one of the tables.

At eleven, Orlando pointed his finger at me. "Kitty and I are going out in the boat," he said, "for a little night-fishing."

"Good for you," I said.

"And you're going to bed."

"Good for me," I said, watching Kitty. I knew she'd

laugh. That was the great thing about her. Then I crossed my fingers. I just had to feed my pigeon first. Max was on his own. He knew where the kitchen goodies were as well as I did.

"What about lace cake for the dessert?" Kitty asked. "To go with my dress?"

We looked at each other, then we both shook our heads.

"Don't move a muscle out of here," Orlando told me and smiled.

I smiled back. "Wait until you see my engagement present." I thought of Bird Berry dancing at the engagement party. "I know you'll love it."

"You're the greatest, Minnie," Orlando said, so I knew he wasn't angry about the bridge anymore. Still, I waited until he was gone five minutes before I spread pigeon food on the restaurant floor for . . .

What was I going to call her anyway? It had to be something to fit with Minnie and Max.

Mischief. That sounded almost like mystery. Good.

I watched Mischief swoop down and peck at the food. She might be just a plain old pigeon, but she was an adorable pigeon. She liked me, too. Her head was bobbing up and down, and she stopped to give me a gentle peck on the ankle.

Then I watched Max devour a plate of blackened scallops. He didn't seem to mind that they were as hard as the stones on Minnow Beach. I was yawning. Suddenly, I couldn't keep my eyes open.

I wandered into my bedroom and fell into bed, telling myself I'd have to get up soon to sweep up the leftover seed.

And then I was singing, *"We're going to get maaar-rried,"* as I listened to the tinkle of the player piano. I could smell something. But with my cold I wasn't sure what it was. Wait a minute.

Music from the player piano?

I sat up straight, mouth dry. Someone had banged into the piano. Max? No. The pigeon? I didn't think so. Maybe Orlando and Kitty? But they wouldn't be back for an hour or two.

Someone was in the restaurant.

I could hear the ruffle of feathers. I could hear Max hiss. I was out of bed and plastered into the corner of the bedroom in one move.

Someone was tiptoeing around in the dining room. A chair scraped; a glass dropped and rolled along on the wooden floor.

I took a step forward, slowly, quietly, but even if I had made a sound, the music was loud enough to cover it. I kept going until I was standing at the edge of the doorway. I peered into the darkness of the dining room, trying to see who it was and where he was. There was the smell of . . . I breathed in. Something. What?

In the dim light from the window, I could see Mischief on the chandelier. Max was harder to spot. But I felt him brush against my legs.

And then I saw the shape. A large shape. I couldn't tell who it was. The clothing was long, loose. A scarf covered his head. Or maybe it was *her* head. Whoever it was stood on the edge of one of the tables, reaching up, reaching for the chandelier. In an instant, I knew what was happening. Someone was trying to steal Mischief.

The person grabbed the edge of the chandelier, holding on for balance, and that's when I moved.

In two giant steps, I was across the room. I pushed the table as hard as I could, watching it topple, and the pigeon flying through to the kitchen. The thief hit the floor.

I began to scream.

10

MICHAEL T. MORIARTY

In nothing flat, Orlando was up out of the boat, barreling into the restaurant. So was every fisherman off Pier Twelve and a couple of guys from the *Owen Stanley* tugboat.

But the pigeon thief was gone.

After everything calmed down, we straightened the tables and swept the floor, Orlando and I. Kitty whipped out her police memo pad, trying to make me remember something about the thief. "Anything," she said.

"It was dark," I said, frowning. "But . . ."

She didn't say anything. She stared at me with her blue eyes, patting my shoulder, waiting as I tried to think of what it was.

"A smell," I said.

"Perfume? Aftershave lotion?"

I closed my eyes.

She patted my hand. "It will come to you, and when it does . . ."

"Bam," I said, "into the slammer."

"Atta girl." She picked up a shard of glass.

Orlando was wringing his hands, wringing his mustache, swearing he'd never leave me for two minutes again for the rest of his life.

"Get a grip," I told him. "The guy wanted the pigeon, not me."

"*You* get a grip, Minnie," he said. "Who'd want a pigeon?"

Indeed. Who'd want Mischief?

I went to bed thinking about it, racking my brains, tossing and turning. Who was the pigeon thief? It had to be someone who thought Mischief was Mary Moon.

Yes, that made sense.

And the only one . . .

I was back to Tough Teresa.

No, two. What about Sonny Breitenback?

And what about that smell?

I closed my eyes, remembering that the *Michael T. Moriarty* was due in Sharkfin Bay tomorrow. I'd get to see Bird Berry, at last. And I'd ask her: Why would Teresa have one of Bird's buttons in her coop?

In the morning I could feel a hint of fall in the air: whitecaps on the bay, the pigeon race signs on Pier Twelve snapping in the wind, clouds rolling in from the east.

And the *Michael T. Moriarty* was rolling in, low in the water, tooting its horn. Cash and Max and I watched from the pier, and Mischief watched from the picnic basket I held on my arm. I wasn't letting her out of my sight for one minute. And the truth was, Mischief didn't seem to want to let us out of her sight either. It was almost as if she had found a home.

Ted was the only one on the boat. I could see that as he tossed the rope onto the pier and hopped off. "I'm sorry, Minnie." He shrugged his shoulders. "I left the letter in the box on her dock. When I came back, the letter was gone, but I didn't see Bird."

"Did you call her?" I asked. "Yell for her?"

"I didn't think of that," he said, yanking on his watch cap.

"Did you go up to her cabin?" Cash asked. I could see he thought Ted was dumb as a sack of rocks.

Ted shook his head. "Didn't think of that, either."

I was angry. I was furious. That Ted of the *Michael T. Moriarty* was useless. "An egg without a yoke," Orlando would say.

We watched Ted hoist a duffel bag to his shoulder, and disappear up Emmons Avenue. And then we looked at each other, Cash and I, Max and Mischief.

"There goes my engagement present for Kitty and Orlando," I said.

Cash was nodding. Max was growling, Mischief was

clucking. Overhead, we could see another pigeon. I think he had his eye on Mischief.

"There's one thing we could do," I said slowly. "Take the—"

"No," Cash said. Cash was a mind reader.

"Take *The Crab's Legs*," I said firmly.

"It's too far," Cash said. "The bay is full of white caps."

". . . and row to Muck Island."

Cash sighed.

"Good," I said. "We have to get our supplies together. Just in case."

"In case what?" Cash said.

Max and Mischief were looking at me.

"In case we get caught in a storm."

11

MUCK ISLAND

All I could think of was that Bird Berry was in trouble. For a moment I wondered if I should tell Kitty and Orlando. But just for a moment. I told myself that Bird had missed seeing the invitation. I tried not to think about accidents and pigeon thieves.

"I'm sure she's all right," I told Cash as we hopped into *The Crab's Legs* a half hour later. I knew I didn't sound so sure.

I thought of Kitty in her pink lace dress.

I thought of Orlando in his blue suit, his dark hair shining.

Yes, Bird had to come to that party. She was Orlando's favorite person—next to me and Kitty, of course.

We cast off a moment later. Tough Teresa was leaning against the pier railing, watching us. "Where are you going?" she asked, slurping up an orange ice pop.

I made believe I was too busy rowing to answer. Max and Cash sat in the stern, and Mischief, in her basket, was perched in the little seat in the bow.

And we had supplies. A Baggie filled with pigeon feed, another filled with Tabby Tidbits, two ham sandwiches on rye with pickles and sliced olives, and a pot for bailing. *The Crab's Legs* was a little leaky.

I could see Sonny fishing on the end dock and Ryan Biale, up in his coop. Actually it was going to be quite an adventure, I thought. My cold was better. I sniffled a little to see. Yes, it was history. No red nose for the party.

As it turned out, it was a good thing we had brought the pot. The water was high, rough, and running fast. And it was much farther to Muck Island than it had seemed when I had taken the *Michael T. Moriarty*. I had only been there once, a couple of years ago when Bird had moved to the island. At first, only Cash was nervous. His face, in between the freckles, looked white.

"Don't worry," I told him.

"I'm not." He pulled the ham sandwich apart and tossed the pickles into a ferocious-looking wave.

"We can see the boats in the bay," I said, trying to reassure myself. "We could call for help if we had to."

I looked over my shoulder as I rowed. Muck Island wasn't getting any closer, but Sharkfin Bay was getting farther away. Much farther. Only the tops of the sailboats were visible now. In the bottom of the boat, water splashed up over my toes.

"Stop eating," I told Cash. "Start bailing."

Cash crouched down. For a moment, the only sound

was the slap of water against the boat and the scrape of the pot.

Then we started to talk. "What have we got?" Cash said.

"A little capsule saying someone is desperate to find his bird."

He looked up at me accusingly. "Too bad the little capsule is back in the water."

"A found pigeon," I went on, ignoring him. "Oh, and Bird's button in Teresa's coop."

"Don't forget, a stuffed pigeon Teresa said was going to win the Pigeon Prize Race on Saturday," Cash said.

I rowed for a minute, trying to think of what else. Muck Island was finally getting closer. I could see the shore ahead of us, the waves rolling in on Bird's small beach. I could see the cabin at the end of the path, and the black-eyed Susans Bird had planted around her doorstep.

I kept thinking about the thief coming into the restaurant. I kept thinking about the smell that night. For the first time, I realized it was the smell of food.

And that's when the boat hit the rock. Hard. Hard enough to toss me off the seat and onto Cash. Hard enough for Mischief's blanket cover to flap back and for Mischief to sail up high over the boat. Hard enough to sweep Max over the side and into the water. Hard enough to tip the boat.

And the next thing I felt was water. In my nose, my ears, my eyes, my mouth. I tried to hold my breath as I went down and down.

And the last thing I thought was that *I* was going to miss Kitty and Orlando's party. I'd never see Kitty in her pink lace dress or Orlando in his new blue suit.

I was going to spoil the most exciting event we had ever had at the Catfish Cafe.

12

MAROONED

I was coughing, sputtering. My ankle was on fire. Someone was rubbing my forehead with sandpaper. Someone else was slapping my face. I opened one eye. "I think I'm alive," I said.

Max stopped licking my forehead; Cash stopped patting my face. Mischief landed on one shoulder.

"Look." Cash pointed toward the dock.

"I think I did something to my ankle," I said.

"Minnie, look," Cash said again.

I sat up slowly. I was on Bird's beach. I could see her trees. I could see Sharkfin Bay, a smudge in the distance. I shaded my eyes. *The Crab's Legs* was floating away.

I could picture Orlando's mustache when he found out. It would be whipping around as if he were in a windstorm. I sighed. We'd have to sell a lot of scallop dinners at the Catfish Cafe to buy another boat.

But Cash was worried about something else. "How will we get out of here?" he asked, chewing on one nail.

"Bird has a boat," I began. "It's bigger than *The Crab's Legs*. She calls it *Big Bird*. Bird will—" I glanced at the dock, at the dark water lapping against it, and shivered. The boat wasn't there.

I tried to scramble up and felt a jolt of pain in my ankle. I wanted to cry. Not because of the ankle so much, but because I was afraid. Bird was gone. We were prisoners on the island.

"Let's try the cabin anyway," Cash said.

With a flutter of wings, Mischief flew to the top of Bird's pigeon loft, and slowly we went up the path, Max shaking himself to get rid of the water in his fur, Cash, head turned, hopping on one foot to get rid of the water in his ears, and I hobbling. We were in trouble.

Bird wasn't in her cabin, of course. We looked around. Pigeon magazines were everywhere, bags of seed littered the table, bird vitamin vials lined the countertops.

It took time to climb to the pigeon loft. I had to make sure Bird wasn't up there; I had to make sure her pigeons were fed. I unlatched the lock on the bottom door and pulled myself up, hand over hand, with Cash one step in back of me.

On top, Cash went inside while I stopped to get my breath. I stopped to look down at my ankle. It looked as if someone had stuffed it with a jar of olives. Red olives, if there were such things.

I heard Cash whistle. "Hey, look at this."

I went inside the loft. But I didn't see what Cash was talking about, at least not at first. All I saw were pigeons, well-fed pigeons with fresh water and food. I saw pigeons with names on their boxes like *Cassiopeia, Jupiter,* and *Big Dipper.*

The sky. The stars. The planets. The firmament.

Cash was looking at me, smiling a little. "Got it?"

"Moon," I said. "Mary Moon. She must be Bird's pigeon."

I ran my tongue over my lips. "And Asteroid."

"What?"

"Asteroid would be one of Bird's pigeons, too," I said. "It fits. Remember . . ."

Cash nodded. "That was the name of one of the birds in Teresa's coop."

I frowned. "Teresa's stealing pigeons all over the place." I sat back. "Just suppose . . ." I began. "Suppose she had stolen Mary Moon. Then somehow Mary escaped—"

"Teresa saw you climbing the bridge," Cash cut in, "and thought the pigeon was Mary Moon . . ."

We watched Mischief pecking at the seeds on the floor.

"Presto," said Cash. "She went into the restaurant to steal her back."

We looked at each other, smiling. What great detectives we were.

Cash shook his head just a little. "But even if she stopped Mary from winning . . ."

55

I sat on Bird's front step, rubbing my ankle. "She certainly couldn't expect to win with Billy the Bird, a stuffed pigeon."

Cash looked smug. "She's got another one, I bet. One she doesn't want anyone to know about."

"Presto," I said. But it wasn't so presto. Mary was still missing, and the truth was, so were we. We'd have to wait a week for the *Michael T. Moriarty* to come around. We'd have to wait while Tough Teresa won the Pigeon Prize Race. Kitty and Orlando would have an engagement party without me.

I shut the door of the pigeon coop, closing in Mischief so she'd be safe, and then we went downstairs to see if we could find some food.

13

MISSION

No food. Not unless you counted salt, pepper, and a bag of lumpy brown sugar. We sat there feeling sorry for ourselves for an hour, as I watched my ankle growing. It was swollen, and throbbing, and all I wanted was to see Kitty and Orlando and sip at one of Orlando's cups of ice-cold tomato soup.

"We're never going to get out of here," Cash said.

"Don't be pathetic," I told him. "Of course we are."

"How?"

"I'm thinking about it right this minute."

And so I started to think. Really think. And came up with the best idea of my life.

I tried to stand up, except that I couldn't stand. Tears came into my eyes. "I've probably broken my ankle in half," I said. "You'll have to do this."

"Do what?" Cash asked, crunching down on a ball of brown sugar.

"Get Mischief down here."

Cash is clever. It didn't take him more than a minute to guess what I was up to. Mischief loved the chandelier in the restaurant. Mischief had been grabbing bits of straw from my beach hat. Mischief was making a nest. Mischief lived at the Catfish Cafe now. It was her loft.

We were sending Mischief on a mission. We were sending her home. I hoped it would work.

I managed to root around in Bird's cabinets, looking for a tiny message capsule. "Sorry, Bird," I told myself. Orlando would skin me alive for going through other people's things. But this was an emergency.

I wrote the message on toilet paper with a stubby little pencil. They were all I could find.

> Mucking around on Muck Island
> Stuck
> Starving
> P.S. Tough Teresa may be tailing us.
> Come fast.
> XXXXXX Max and Minnie and Cash

We tucked Mischief into her harness, talking to her all the time. "Go straight home. Don't stop on a bridge. Don't get caught by Tough Teresa. Find Orlando. Find Kitty."

Max meowed in agreement. He wasn't going to last long on salt, pepper, and brown sugar.

We stood outside Bird's cabin and gave Mischief a little toss, then we watched as she flew, up, straight, high, heading over the water like an arrow. Straight for Sharkfin Bay. Straight for the Catfish Cafe, I hoped.

And then we sat down to wait.

And wait.

14

MAD DASH

And then it was dark. Really dark. Once in a while we'd see a pinpoint of light in the distance. I guess we wouldn't have felt so terrible if we were sure Mischief would reach the Catfish Cafe. "She has to have made it by now," I said. "Pigeons won't fly at night."

I sat there sucking on brown sugar bits, and sniffling over my sore ankle. Then I began to think about the smell of food in the restaurant that night. Not our food. Something else.

Teresa was always eating.

And what about Sonny Breitenback with his cloves of garlic smelling like a pesto pizza?

I played around with that for a bit, but then I shook my head. Sonny was into tumblers, not racers. It was Tough Teresa. It had to be Teresa.

I tried to make myself feel better by thinking about my gorgeous purple outfit, and what we might serve for dessert at the engagement party. Maybe that's why I didn't see the boat as soon as Cash did. "Minnie," he said. "I think we're saved."

I pulled myself up off the porch step to see better. What I saw was a nightmare. "It's Tough Teresa," I said.

Cash dived in back of a bush.

Even with my ankle twice its usual size, I grabbed Max, crawled in under the cabin, and pulled Max's tail in after me. Teresa was after us, after Mischief. Lucky for Mischief she wasn't Mary Moon. Lucky for Mischief she was safe at the Catfish Cafe.

And then Teresa was calling. "Minnie," she yelled. "Cash." She even started with a "Here, kitty, kitty, kitty, kitty."

None of us moved. None of us even breathed.

We heard her footsteps on Bird's wooden steps, heard her open the door and close it again. She tried another "Here, kitty," then headed for the pigeon loft.

It was hard to follow her without making any noise. Actually it was impossible. She heard me and turned around. "Minnie?" she called.

I didn't answer her. Of course, I didn't. I was plastered against one of Bird's trees with Max in my arms.

She mumbled something, then opened the door to the loft stairs.

I didn't care if she heard me then. I had enough time to

lock her inside. I had enough time to hear that there was another boat coming. I had enough time to know that we were saved. I wasn't even worried when I heard her carrying on, yelling, and banging the loft door like crazy.

But, of course, we weren't saved. All the clues we had been adding up were wrong. Between the two of us, Cash and I didn't even equal one detective.

Because the other boat wasn't Kitty in the police boat. It wasn't Orlando. But I didn't know that. I hopped down to the dock, thinking about how hungry I was, hoping that Orlando had brought a little snack for us, a cookie or two, or a Hershey's bar. Then there was a click in my head and all the pieces slid into place.

Chocolate, the smell had been chocolate.

The pigeon thief had to be Ryan Biale. Ryan who had said he was determined to win the pigeon race.

Now he was tossing the rope over the piling. Was he on his way up to get us?

And I, who could hardly walk, had about two minutes to find Cash and let Tough Teresa out of the pigeon loft.

I did it in a minute and a half. I flipped up the hook on the door and whispered for Cash as loud as I could. Then with Max in my arms, with Cash on one side and Teresa on the other, we made a mad dash through the trees and collapsed into Teresa's boat. At the last minute, Cash reached out and pulled the loop of rope from Ryan's boat off the piling. We watched it floating away.

And then we were gone, before Ryan had reached Bird Berry's cabin, out on the water, the noise of Teresa's motor ringing in our ears.

"Just tell me," I asked her as we headed back toward Sharkfin Bay, "how did you think a stuffed bird named Billy the Kid was going to win the race?"

Teresa started to laugh. "We knew there was a thief," she said. "We knew he wanted to get rid of any pigeon who might beat his pigeon, so we set a trap. We kept talking about my great pigeon, Billy. We knew he'd come."

"But we came instead," I said, nodding.

"And you were too fast for us," said Teresa.

"You keep saying *we*," I said, "and *us*."

Teresa blinked. "Bird, of course. Bird Berry. We're a team. We had been sending messages back and forth, using the pigeons." She grinned at us. "Bird had come in from the island. She was hiding in the coop that night." She shook her head. "Too bad she fell asleep."

For a moment we were quiet. In the distance I could hear another motor. I closed my eyes. Kitty and Orlando, I knew it, probably in the police boat.

We were really saved.

I blinked. What was Max doing, curled up in Teresa's lap?

"I thought you hated cats," I said.

Teresa nodded. "Max was there that night, smooching around Bird. He's actually a terrific cat."

I nodded. There was one thing left to do. Get Mary Moon. And then it hit me. Could Mischief be Mary Moon after all? I knew where she was. She was in the chandelier at the Catfish Cafe. I swallowed. How could Max and I give her up?

We had no choice. The race was tomorrow.

15

MARY MOON

We slopped ourselves out of Tough Teresa's boat and headed toward the Catfish Cafe, with Max stopping for a quick bite of fish bait on the front walk.

Inside, Mischief was staring down at us, a piece of my straw hat in her mouth. And that's when Orlando and Kitty walked in. Orlando could hardly talk. He threw himself onto a chair, huffing and puffing and patting his poor mustache into place. "How could you do this to us, Minnie?" he asked. "I thought you were dead."

"Or worse," I said.

Kitty grinned. Then she patted Orlando's back.

I watched a bit of straw float down and settle in a water glass. Then I pointed toward Mischief. "May I present Mary Moon?" I said, in my best stage-actress voice. I hoped no one heard the quiver. I really loved that pigeon, almost as much as Max.

But I didn't have time to think about that.

"That's not Mary Moon," Teresa said. "Not by a long shot."

Orlando looked up. "Bad enough in the bedroom. But a pigeon in the restaurant? On top of the tables? Tables all gussied up with pink cloths for the party tomorrow. The restaurant's best glasses, polished . . ."

"Not the greatest spot for a pigeon, but we can find another . . ." Kitty began, trying to smooth everything over.

"Not Mary Moon," I said, feeling great, feeling wonderful, feeling like the world's worst detective.

"A half-grown pigeon," said Teresa. "She could make it from Muck Island to here. And that's if she had to. But she'd be tired. She won't be ready for a long race for a while."

"I love this pigeon," Kitty said. "She brought the message straight home to us."

I thought about that, and then I thought about something else. I drew myself up. "I think I know where Mary Moon is."

Cash was nodding. "Yes," he said. "Your cold."

"Presto," I said.

"What now?" asked Orlando.

Kitty smiled at him. "Give them a moment. They're figuring it out. It's what detectives do."

I swallowed. That Kitty was the best. Cash and I looked at each other. "Mary Moon is in Ryan Biale's loft." And once I said it I knew I was right. I wondered how we didn't think of it sooner.

"He wouldn't let us in," Cash said. "He said Minnie had a cold."

"Pigeons don't catch colds from people," said Tough Teresa.

Kitty raised her hand. "This is where I come in," she said. "You need a police person."

We all nodded. We waited until Kitty called the Sixty-first Precinct for backup. And then she was off to Muck Island to nab Ryan Biale.

"He's not going to win the race," I said.

"Not by a long shot," said Tough Teresa.

I still had some thinking to do. I sat there, eyes closed, trying to follow it through. Ryan had stolen Mary. Yes. He was hiding her so she couldn't win. Right. But then he had heard me say Mischief was fast. He couldn't take a chance on her being faster than his pigeon. So he had come after her. Twice. Once in the restaurant. Once on the island.

Presto.

It was only a few hours later that I went with Kitty to rescue Mary Moon, and to see her, at last.

She looked like a regular pigeon, except for her eyes. She had beautiful eyes, shiny and friendly, and you just knew by looking at her that tomorrow she'd win the race for Bird Berry.

That's when I thought about my engagement present, and the party. "What about dessert?"

At the same time, Kitty was talking about Ryan. "I fingerprinted him myself," she said.

And that's when I thought of what dessert we'd make. Except that we'd be up all night.

And then one more thing, whose pigeon was Mischief?

16

MOONBEAM

It was hot in the kitchen. The stove was going full blast, and Kitty was dressed up in pink lace. I was in my purple outfit, with a huge bandage on one ankle. We were putting jelly in the fingerprint cookies—the perfect dessert for a cop and a cook. Next to us, Orlando was slipping the hot cookies onto the plates. And underneath, Max and Mischief were scarfing up the rejects.

I peeked out of the kitchen door. The restaurant was filling up with guests. Cash and the rest of his family were there, Cash wearing a jacket and tie. Everyone else from Sharkfin Bay was there, too. But I was looking for just one person.

And there she was, wearing a long flowing dress with one button missing. She smiled when she saw me.

I was smiling, too. "Bird," I whispered, beckoning to her.

And, once again in my actress voice, I said, "Ta-da, my engagement present."

Orlando stepped back. "Wow," he said. "Wow, Minnie. Wow, Bird."

Then I watched everyone hugging Bird. Then she hugged Orlando and Kitty, then me. I listened as everyone said Bird was the greatest present in the entire world.

And then, the best news of all. Bird looked down at Mischief. "It's Moonbeam," she said. "Mary Moon's daughter."

I swallowed. "Your pigeon?"

"Yours now," she said. "My engagement gift to the Catfish Cafe."

And then it was time to get the party started. With Kitty on one side, and Orlando on the other, I took a moment to press A-2 on the piano.

"A love song," said Cash.

I shook my head. It was "Pet-toon-ya You're My Piddgg-yonn."

"Why not?" said Orlando.

"Right," said Kitty.

I just smiled. What a day. The party and the pigeon race. After we had dinner, we'd go over to Muck Island to watch Mary Moon come in first.

Minnie's Fingerprint Cookies
(Make with an adult)

½ pound butter or margarine
2 cups sifted flour
½ cup sugar
jar of strawberry jelly (You'll have some left . . . if you
don't eat it all while you're cooking.)

1. In a large bowl, mix everything together but the jelly,
until it's nice and fluffy.
2. Shape into olive-sized balls.
3. Put the balls of dough about an inch apart on an un-
greased baking sheet.
4. Press your finger into the top of each ball to make an in-
dentation. Then fill the indentations with jelly.
5. Bake at 375 degrees for about ten minutes or until the
cookies are brown on the bottom.
6. Use a spatula to remove the cookies from the sheet.
Makes about three dozen cookies.